LAND
OF THE
GODS

SALLY PRUE

BLOOMSBURY EDUCATION
AN IMPRINT OF BLOOMSBURY
LONDON OXFORD NEW YORK NEW DELHI SYDNEY

First published 2016 by Bloomsbury Education, an imprint of
Bloomsbury Publishing Plc

50 Bedford Square, London, WC1B 3DP

www.bloomsbury.com

Bloomsbury is a registered trademark of Bloomsbury Publishing Plc

A CIP catalogue for this book is available from the British Library

ISBN: 978-1-4729-1809-3 (paperback)

Typeset by Newgen Knowledge Works (P) Ltd., Chennai, India
Printed and bound by CPI Group (UK) Ltd, Croydon CR0 4YY

1 3 5 7 9 10 8 6 4 2

CONTENTS

CHAPTER ONE

A buzzard screamed. I leapt a foot in the air and woke up.

The shadows had lengthened, and that meant I was going to be in really deep trouble with Uncle Vertigern. I scrambled up in a hurry and I was just going to throw myself down the hillside towards home when a glint of something in the valley caught my eye.

I spared just a moment to look – then I looked again – and then I threw myself back down flat on the ground.

That buzzard probably saved my life, because if I'd been spotted I'd have been done for. There was a bit of scrubby thorn bush a little way away so I wriggled over on my belly, squirmed behind it, and tried to look like a rock.

The ground was trembling. By the gods, they were heavy – a file of men, made even heavier by their armour and weapons. I winced, and tried not to think about their weapons. I was huddled into a ball, but that left my back horribly exposed. I was desperate to check that no one was about to drive a spear into me but I knew I mustn't move.

They were getting close. I tried to work out how many of them there were, but I'd only got the smallest glimpse. Perhaps sixty, I thought: sixty Roman soldiers in a column, two by two, with their curved shields catching the light and giving them away.

I heard a voice. I knew Latin because Mother had taught me, but the nearness of the voice threw me into such sheer terror – I mean

8

surprise – that it robbed me of my wits. I pressed my face into the mud and prayed fervent prayers to all the gods: to the Hawthorn Queen, and to Rhiannon, and to Lug of the Long Arm. I lay there and reminded them of all the sacrifices I'd ever made them, and I grovelled.

Always be polite to powerful people – especially if they're gods.

The Romans were only a matter of feet away now and the bush felt as if it had shrunk to the size of a mushroom. All my instincts were telling me to run away, or yell, or jump up – anything – and I was horribly afraid I was going to lose my head and do all of those things. That wasn't the only thing I was horribly afraid of. What if one of the soldiers needed to go behind a bush? I wasn't actually sure if Romans *did* go behind bushes; all I knew about Romans was that they loved killing people.

I stayed where I was, quivering, until I was sure the Romans had gone by. Then I pulled my nose out of the mud and wriggled forward a little bit so I could peer after them. They said that Romans always marched in a straight line, but it wasn't true because they'd changed direction.

Now they were heading for the homestead.

I turned round and began to crawl, and then, when it was safe, I got up and ran – and, let's face it, I couldn't have done anything more sensible if I'd sat down and thought about it for a week. You know what Romans are like.

I ran right over the top of the ridge and then down into the next valley. All I thought about was getting as far away from those Romans as I could. It wasn't so much that I was scared – I mean, I'm really brave – but seeing them in real life made me realise just how much being stabbed by one of their spears would *hurt*.

It wasn't long before I'd gone further than I'd ever gone before, and after that I had to let the gods guide me: odds left, evens right. When it got dark, a freezing, soaking mist rolled down from the hills. Now, I'm ever so strong – cousin

Cattigern says I'm fat, but it's not fat: it's all muscle – but even so, in the end, I got to the stage where I was so tired I was practically walking in my sleep. If I hadn't set off some dogs barking, I would probably have plodded on until morning.

If there were dogs, there were people. But what sort of people? If they were Romans I was done for: they'd tear me apart, bit by bit, and enjoy doing it. But then if they were the wrong tribe of Britons I was done for, too.

I'd almost decided to walk on when the moon came out and I saw there was a covered wagon by the side of the track. It looked deserted, so I stole up to it and listened.

Nothing.

I knew that hanging round that wagon was stupidly dangerous, but it was either shelter in there or freeze half to death. And there didn't seem to be anyone about. I heaved myself up over the tailboard. The wagon was loaded with rolls of cloth, and it was wonderful to get out of the biting wind. I allowed myself to relax, just for a minute.

I was really tired, but I was in so much danger that only a fool would have been stupid enough to fall asleep.

CHAPTER TWO

Someone shouted. I sort of heard them, but it wasn't until someone got hold of me and dragged me out into the cold air that I really woke up, and even then I only thought it was Uncle Vertigern. I blinked up at him, trying to think of excuses.

But it wasn't my uncle. It was someone with short hair and no moustache. That meant he was a Roman.

I was dead meat.

'Who are you?' he demanded, but I was too appalled to get my voice to work.

'Aphrodisius!' the man bawled, his hand like a vice on my arm. 'Who's this?'

A bony man in dirty clothes slid round the end of the wagon. He fluttered apprehensive eyes.

'A Celt, Master Balbus,' he said apologetically.

Balbus gave him a hefty whack with his stick. The worst thing was that I winced more than Aphrodisius did.

'What's he doing in here?'

'I – I can't tell you, Master Balbus.'

Then Balbus whacked Aphrodisius again and bellowed a lot, but he never once let go of me. He was a big man with bulging eyes, and he was so strong that struggling was a waste of time.

And so I was going to die.

Balbus got tired of ranting and raving quite soon – it was still quite early in the morning –

and then he turned his attention to me. By then my brain had woken up, and in spite of everything I'd worked out an extremely clever story. I was a slave of the Roman chief at Viroconium, and I'd got lost returning home after taking a message. That was a really *good* lie – I mean, there really was a Roman fort called Viroconium and everything – and the only trouble with it was that Balbus didn't believe it for a minute. Balbus didn't even think it was worth whacking me for. He just joined my wrist to Aphrodisius's with a pair of metal rings and prowled off to see about getting the wagon under way.

Well, all I could think of for ages was, *Thank all the gods he didn't kill me*. The next thing I thought about was getting out of there. I spent ages trying to wriggle my hand out of the metal ring but it was so obviously hopeless that Aphrodisius didn't even bother to watch.

'Where are you going to take me?' I asked, when I was tired of scraping the skin off my wrist.

'Down to the coast, I expect,' said Aphrodisius, gloomily. 'Through Gaul, probably. Dalmatia, Rome, Macedonia – who knows?'

I let out a yelp.

'But that's right across the world! I can't go all that way!'

Aphrodisius had a long, mournful, long-suffering face, like a bloodhound, but he smiled woodenly, as if he'd almost forgotten how. He lifted his hand and my wrist lifted with it.

'I don't think you've got a lot of choice about that,' he said.

CHAPTER THREE

The track was stony, and the first thing I found out when we started walking along behind the wagon was that I'd got a blister on my heel.

'What will Balbus do to me?' I asked, pathetically, as I limped along.

Aphrodisius shrugged.

'Sell you,' he said.

I'd let out a howl before I knew what I was doing, because I knew what happened to slaves. 'It's not fair!' I said. 'Why do the Romans always cut the heads off the strong, clever, good-looking ones when they're making sacrifices to their gods?'

'They don't,' said Aphrodisius. 'Roman gods don't go in for human sacrifices.'

But that was even worse, because if you didn't slit slaves' throats on an altar then the odds were that you stuffed them into a wickerwork cage and set fire to them.

I howled again at the injustice of it.

'No, no,' said Aphrodisius. 'No, Romans don't do that sort of thing. That's just you savage Celts.' I could hardly bear to ask, but I just had to know.

'What *do* the Romans do with slaves, then?'

Aphrodisius really enjoyed telling people bad news, blast him. Some slaves got sent down the mines: a cruel, dirty and short life. Others got sent to the circus to be torn apart by bears, or else, if you were lucky enough to end up in a big place, by lions.

I howled some more. All that talent, thrown to a wild beast. What a *waste*.

Or some slaves worked in the fields, starved and frozen, with only a stone hut to live in.

I didn't howl at that, partly because my throat was getting sore, and partly because that didn't sound too bad. It fact, it sounded just like home.

'Here,' I said, suddenly realising something. 'Aren't *you* a slave?'

Aphrodisius nodded mournfully.

'It's no life,' he said. 'Beaten, treated like a beast of burden, sent hither and yon.' But as he said it the scent of garlic on his breath hit me. Garlic. I *liked* garlic.

I thought a lot, as I plodded on. The Romans had caught me, and everyone knew they were the nastiest, cruellest, most savage people in the whole world. The stories I'd heard about the Romans were enough to make your hair stand on end and your eyes pop out.

But then...

... Aphrodisius seemed to manage and, let's face it, he didn't have half my intelligence or looks.

Well, the main thing was that I was alive.

For the moment.

SUL

CHAPTER FOUR

We came off the track just as it was beginning to get dark and climbed up onto a raised causeway covered with gravel.

'They put these roads everywhere, the Romans do,' said Aphrodisius. 'It's no good running away or rebelling: a legion of soldiers can march thirty miles a day along these things.' Aphrodisius wasn't much of a laugh.

We kept on until long after dark. I never got to see anything of the place where we stopped because Balbus handcuffed me to one of the roof-struts of the wagon for the night. It was freezing.

I was just deciding that I wasn't going to live long enough to be sold when Balbus turned up with a large white cloak and threw it at me. Then he burped, and wandered off.

I showed the cloak to Aphrodisius. It had a purple border, and when I shook it out I found a gold pendant within the folds. I was so astonished that for a moment I wondered if Balbus had been won over by my beauty, charm and intelligence, and had decided to adopt me. I was just thinking that Balbus couldn't be any more horrible than Uncle Vertigern – who wasn't really my uncle at all, but just someone who'd taken me in when Mother died – when Aphrodisius went and spoiled everything.

'That's not a cloak, it's a toga,' he said. 'The toga praetexta. Roman children wear them.'

I'd heard of togas: stupid, impractical, wraparound sheet things that even the Romans only wore for swaggering about.

'And what's this?' I asked, holding up the little golden ball on its chain.

'Roman children wear them, too.'

I was still puzzled, but I wasn't complaining. I mean, whatever Balbus's reasons were, at that moment looking like a Roman was a lot safer than looking like a Celt.

'It's so Balbus doesn't have to pay any tax on you,' Aphrodisius explained. 'If people think you're a Roman, Balbus won't have to pay any slave tax.'

I should have known. Of course Balbus wasn't a kindly old man who wanted to adopt me as his son. Balbus was a greedy, cheating, no-good villain.

And I was utterly, completely, and absolutely in his power.

We spent that day trudging miles behind the wagon until at last we came to a river. I'd never seen so many people as there were in that place: there were men with metal hooks loading bales and crates onto barges, and people making marks in trays of wax, and all the time a babble of voices and lots of pushing and shoving.

Balbus made me put the toga on. I kept my own tunic on underneath it, and it was a good thing I did, because I just couldn't get the hang of how to stop my toga falling down. You had to hold the thing up all the time with your left arm, and even then it kept slipping off your shoulder. I stood there shivering in the stiff breeze and I didn't half miss my trousers, I can tell you. Still, at least I didn't have to help load the barge. It was quite fun watching Aphrodisius puffing and straining.

The barge was worrying. Instead of being made of a hollowed tree trunk like a proper, Celtic boat, it was made of planks of wood fixed together with metal nails. I prayed like mad to the river goddess Deva, because anyone with half a brain could see that the thing was going to sink as soon as it left the wharf. But the Roman gods must have put a spell on it, I think – because, as it turned out, the thing hardly leaked at all.

We travelled on the barge all day and all night. I suppose it beat walking. Balbus had no choice but to take my handcuffs off as he was pretending I was a Roman, and if I'd been able to swim then perhaps I could have escaped. There were a few other passengers, mostly Celts from tribes that had been conquered by the Romans.

When the sun came up, the river had widened so much I thought it was the sea. *Goodbye Britain*, I thought. But then after a couple of hours we turned into another river. We were going against the current this time, but they hoisted a cloth to catch the wind and with the help of every slave at the oars – except me – we managed to make progress.

By about dinner time we came to another wharf, and this time Balbus took a firm hold of my wrist and led me over the gangplank onto land. I was so stiff by then that moving was agony. Of course, I got caught up in the folds of my blasted toga and nearly put my foot through it. Balbus walloped me for carelessness, but I was so numb from sitting on the hard wooden seat that I didn't feel it.

'Where are we?' I asked Aphrodisius, as we waited for our part of the cargo to be unloaded. Everywhere was knee-deep in mud, but there were queues of barges on the river waiting to land big cubes of rock.

'This is the Spring of Sul.'

Wow. The Spring of Sul. I tucked up my toga and squatted down to kiss the mud straight away, because Sul is one of the most powerful goddesses in the whole of Britain. Why, she cured Uncle Vertigern of his rheumatism last summer, and he'd only sacrificed a weakly little billy goat. Good value, that was, because the pain was making him ever so bad-tempered.

Now, if I could only find some excuse for visiting the Spring, I could send a prayer straight to Sul and she'd have me free in no time.

CHAPTER FIVE

Balbus prowled over. It was drizzling, and I missed my trousers more than ever.

'Curse this rain,' he growled. 'It makes my head split.'

It was more likely that staying up half the night partying with the boatmen was making his head split. But I didn't say so because I'd had a stroke of genius.

Which happens quite often, with me.

'Sul will cure you,' I said. 'If I visit the Spring then I could pray to her for you, if you like. She'll take special notice of me as I'm a Celt.'

Balbus harrumphed – but then winced as he jarred his head.

'Oh, I suppose it's worth a try,' he said. 'But don't think you're going to get a chance to escape.'

And he yelled for Aphrodisius.

The Spring was incredible: so full of magic you could smell it. Why, the water actually rose hot and steaming straight from the ground. I tried to think strong, holy thoughts so that my prayers would be extra powerful, but it was difficult to concentrate because Aphrodisius kept sniggering. Balbus had given him ten denarii as an offering to Sul – talk about the last of the big spenders – and, of course, Aphrodisius was planning to spend them stuffing himself.

Honestly, if anyone really deserved to be a slave, it was Aphrodisius.

'Sul will blast you,' I pointed out. 'She'll shrivel you up until you're screaming in agony, and then she'll have you torn apart by wild beasts.'

But he was too stupid to listen.

Outside the Spring, the Romans were using teams of oxen to pull the blocks of stone along to a place where they were building. There wasn't much to see, yet, except mud, which my stupid Roman sandals let straight through. A little way away from the building site there were stalls set up, so we squelched our way over to have a look. It was mostly animals for sacrificing, but there was a hawk-nosed man with big ears who was sitting surrounded by little squares of metal that he was writing on with a sharp stick.

'What's this?' I asked.

The man barely looked up.

'Curse-making service,' he muttered.

And Aphrodisius, the fool, suddenly looked quite gloriously happy. He slapped Balbus's ten denarii on the table and began working out a thoroughly nasty curse.

I want to make it clear that I had nothing to do with laying that curse. Aphrodisius thought he was being incredibly clever and cunning to get Balbus to pay to put a curse on himself, but personally I didn't like it a bit. I went down to the sacred Spring and stared at myself in the water. Balbus had given me a Roman haircut to go with my clothes, but apart from the cold ears I didn't mind, because I'm so handsome I always look good.

'Sul,' I whispered – I knew she'd listen, because the gods love beautiful people – 'oh most lovely and powerful goddess, bless me. Keep me safe, and help me to escape before the Romans kill me. I swear that I'll make you offerings as soon as I can, and I swear that you shall be my special goddess, just as Lug is my special god. Oh, and will you cure Balbus's headache, please, if it's not too much trouble? Because it makes him bad-tempered and then he hits me. Hear me, oh great and lovely Sul.'

Aphrodisius's face appeared in the sacred water next to mine and I got up hastily so my reflection wouldn't be in the pool when the curse entered it. Aphrodisius chucked in the curse without so much as a bow or a prayer.

Aphrodisius was a fool to mess about with his master, and even more of a fool to mess about with the gods.

Well, he paid for it.

Balbus was fuming by the time we got back. He walloped us both hard, and then we left Sul's Spring along another fine Roman road.

Aphrodisius and I trudged along behind the wagon for four days. At one point we took a turning east, but mostly we just walked and walked and walked. Sometimes we passed other traffic: wagons, and travellers on horseback or on foot. Most of the travellers were Celts – Belgae or Atrobates, they must have been – but lots of them had shaved their moustaches and cut their hair. They looked sleek and very well fed. I'd noticed that the fields were ploughed deeply even in the heaviest soil. The Romans must have brought in some new sort of plough. They were clever, those Romans.

On the morning of the fourth day, Balbus told me to put my toga on again. It was lucky I'm right-handed, because once you'd got your toga on you couldn't really use your left hand.

We walked on, and about mid-morning the traffic began to get heavier, and a little while later we saw a procession coming along. It was led by horn players and sour-sounding flutes, and when we got level with them, we could see that they had a dead man on a litter. There was a whole crowd of people behind who were wailing and screaming. It was really spooky and horrible, and my flesh was still creeping ten minutes later when we came to a big mound and a ditch. Aphrodisius said we'd come to a thing called a *town*.

The town was called Calleva Atrebatum, and it was... how can I describe it? It was incredible, and amazing, and gob-smacking, and out of this world, and – and I didn't even *think* about closing my mouth for ages. There were *dozens* of buildings, and they weren't round stone huts with mud to fill in the gaps, either. These buildings had straight, smooth walls, and roofs covered in squares of pottery. It was – it was just incredible. Some of those buildings had three rows of windows, as if the rooms inside were stacked up on top of one another. I was so utterly gob-smacked that I wouldn't have been surprised to see Romans *flying* up to those top windows.

I prayed like mad to Lug and Sul, I can tell you.

We parked the wagon, and then Balbus told me to take my toga off again so I folded it up and put it over my shoulder and tied it on with my belt, and then we got down to work. We carried some bales of cloth down a road – they had proper roads, even inside the town – and then left past a cattle pen.

And there was the house of the gods.

LUG

CHAPTER SIX

It scared me, to tell you the truth. I mean, I'm really brave, but it was the biggest man-made thing I'd ever seen, and the tallest man-made thing I'd ever seen. It ran the whole length of the road, and in the middle was a square opening, held up on pillars.

I would much rather have stayed outside, but Balbus chivvied us through the opening and into a square surrounded by buildings – and then I realised it couldn't be the house of the gods after all, because it was full of people jostling each other and buying things.

We started setting out our wares on an empty stall. Aphrodisius did, anyway. My eyes were practically falling off their stalks and it was as much as I could do to remember to breathe from time to time. The most unnerving thing was that most of the people in the place were British. Why had the Romans let so many Celts into the town? And why weren't they all killing each other?

Balbus gave me a clip round the ear to wake me up, but just then a man came out from the arched doorway of the tallest building of all, and he was so... so... so *splendid* that I couldn't have taken my eyes off him for anything. He was a soldier, but he was even bigger and shinier than the other Roman soldiers I'd seen. He wore gleaming armour. He held a staff in his hand, and had tall plumes on his helmet.

Aphrodisius noticed him at the same time as I did. Aphrodisius gave him an appalled look, squeaked, and dived behind the table. Balbus was busy assuring a customer that she'd not find finer cloth if she travelled all the way to Carthage, so he didn't notice the soldier.

But the shiny man noticed Balbus. He stopped, frowned, and then swung round towards us, his bronze armour flashing. It was too late to throw myself under the table with Aphrodisius so I made myself as small as I could and I prayed some more to Sul and Lug.

'Balbus!'

Balbus's head jerked round at the soldier's voice and his sales talk died in his mouth. He was struck with such horror that he froze for a moment, but then he recovered himself and spread his face with a smile of buttery welcome.

'Noble Centurion,' he said, bowing low. 'Your worship, Sabidus Maximus. I thought you would be with the valiant Second Legion in Isca Silurum. What a surprise and pleasure.'

The centurion gave half a grim smile.

'A surprise, anyway,' he said. 'It's very convenient.'

Balbus blinked rapidly, trying to work that out.

'You need cloth?' he hazarded. 'I have some fine wool here. You won't find finer cloth if you were to go all the way to –'

The centurion put his hand on the sheath of his broad-bladed dagger, and Balbus's voice died away in a gulp.

'Ah, Balbus, but I've done business with you before, don't forget,' said Sabidus Maximus, quietly. 'I bought some rations for my men from you. Do you remember?'

Balbus's bulging eyes were fixed on Sabidus's hand, which was still resting on the hilt of his dagger. Balbus had to swallow before he could speak.

'Finest grain,' he said. But his voice had a pleading edge to it. 'Best quality –'

'– sand,' said the centurion, crushingly. 'Ten sacks of grain, and ten sacks of sand.'

Balbus raised his hands to the sky.

'I am innocent!' he cried. 'By all the gods I swear it!'

I stepped back hastily in case Balbus was struck by lightning for telling a lie, but Aphrodisius was scuttling away under the cover of the table, and I accidentally stood on his hand.

The centurion ignored Aphrodisius's howl. He was looking faintly bored. Balbus tried again.

'Someone must have tampered with it after I sold it to you,' he said. 'I call upon all the gods, upon the emperor himself, to judge me!'

Why Balbus wasn't struck down then I don't know. Perhaps the Roman emperor-god happened to be busy doing other things, or perhaps he didn't want to soil his hands on Balbus, or perhaps he knew what was going to happen next.

'Can't quite manage the emperor,' said the centurion, drily. 'But the chief magistrate's in the basilica. We'll lay the matter before him, I think.'

Balbus looked at the centurion's dagger, and his face went as white as chalk. Then he drew himself up, squared his shoulders, and allowed the centurion to usher him into the very tallest and most god-like building of all.

And as he was passing me, Balbus reached out a large hand and took me with him, too.

CHAPTER SEVEN

The basilica was completely unbelievable. Amazing.

Remember, the only building I'd ever been in was a round hut made of piled-up stones, and this place... well, it was massive, for a start. I reckon it must have been eighty paces long and twenty across, and it was nearly as high as it was wide. It had two great lines of columns down the middle, all decorated with leafy carving. It had...

... But it would take forever to describe the panels of veined stone, and the bright colours, and the great rafters; it was so gob-smacking I really did wonder if this might be the house of the gods.

At one end of the place, on a great chair, was a man in a purple-bordered toga just like mine. Aphrodisius had said that my sort of toga was for children, but this man wasn't young. On his face were carved deep, sour lines, and practically all the hair he had was sprouting from his nostrils.

He might have been bald, but he must have been really important because even the centurion bowed. Balbus almost banged his nose on the floor.

Well, it was obvious from the start that Balbus was going to be found guilty. I mean, Sabidus Maximus was a centurion and Balbus was a merchant: no contest. The magistrate (the man in the chair was apparently the magistrate) did listen to both of them, but as he'd once bought some cloth from Balbus that'd turned out to be moth-eaten, Balbus had no chance.

'Guilty,' said the magistrate, with some satisfaction. 'Will you pay the fine, Balbus, or will you be sold into slavery?'

'Oh, I'll pay, Tammonius Vitalis, I'll pay,' said Balbus, hastily. 'I'll sell one of my own slaves to raise the money.'

'Won't be enough,' snapped Tammonius. 'Officer of the court!'

'Two slaves,' Balbus amended, in a hurry. 'This one here, look,' he said, dragging me forward from where I was pretending to be an innocent bystander. 'He's strong, good-looking, intelligent. He'll fetch a good price. I was planning to take him to Rome, but in the present circumstances – I can see how appearances have conspired against me – I surrender him to the court.'

The magistrate peered at me, and my heart started beating fast. Sold? Now? Who would buy me? And what for?

Tammonius turned to scowl at Balbus.

'He's not a slave,' he said. 'He has Nundina's charm round his neck.'

I hadn't known my gold pendant, which I'd forgotten to take off with my toga, was a charm. I whispered a prayer to Nundina, whoever

42

she was: *Please don't let them sell me to the circus!*

Balbus tried to laugh.

'I am a kind master,' he said. 'I was afraid the boy would... would come to some harm. So I dressed him as a Roman.'

Tammonius Vitalis raised an eyebrow.

'It wasn't to avoid paying tax on him, then?'

'No! By all the gods I swear it!' said Balbus.

I suppose he thought he was safe from lightning because of the tiled roof. The magistrate regarded him beadily.

'If the boy has Nundina's charm, then he has her protection,' he said. 'And if I'm not mistaken that's a sacred toga praetexta the boy's got over his shoulder, and that also gives him rights.' He smoothed down his own toga over his belly and looked smug. 'The judgement of the court,' he announced, 'is that by dressing this boy as a Roman you have made him a Roman. He is free, and cannot be sold to pay your fine.'

Free? I thought. I was too surprised to believe it. Balbus believed it. He sagged.

'I have a wagon-load of cloth that could be sold,' he said glumly. Tammonius nodded. 'Very well. Officer of the court!'

So Balbus stomped off with the officer of the court. I didn't know what to do. It was great being free, except that I was a hundred miles from home, if home hadn't been destroyed by that column of Roman soldiers. And even if it *was* still there, well, it hadn't been much of a home, anyway. In any case, I had no work and no food and I didn't know the way. What *could* I do?

CHAPTER EIGHT

Tammonius saw me standing there and waved an irritable finger at me.

'Centurion!' he snapped. 'Sabidus Maximus!'

The centurion stopped halfway to the door.

'Sir?'

'The boy.'

The centurion looked blank.

'The boy, sir?'

'You heard me,' said Tammonius, tetchily. 'I don't want him hanging about. He gawps. Take him away at once.'

The centurion took a step forward and then stopped.

'Take him away where, sir?'

Tammonius made a shooing motion.

'*I* don't know!' he exclaimed. 'He came with you, didn't he? He's your responsibility. Where are you posted?'

The centurion's face settled into a deeply grim expression.

'Isca Silurum, sir,' he said stiffly.

'Then take him there. Anywhere, as long as I'm not tripping over him. Now be off with both of you!'

The centurion hesitated, but then he bowed and strode off, and I followed him as fast as I could. Everyone in the market square made haste to get out of the centurion's way. I was keeping up with him quite well, but then when I was nearly at the gateway Aphrodisius popped up from nowhere and grabbed me.

'What happened?' he demanded.

I hadn't time to break it to him gently.

46

'Balbus was found guilty and you and the wagon are to be sold to pay his fine.'

Aphrodisius went so pale that all his dirt showed up quite distinctly.

'What am I going to *do?*' he wailed.

'Run away,' I suggested. He shuddered and shook his head.

'They'd hunt me down,' he whimpered. 'But then if I stay they'll sell me to the mines – or to the circus! What can I do? What can I *do?*'

My centurion was passing through the gate and if I stopped any longer I was going to lose him altogether.

'Pray,' I said to Aphrodisius, and shook him off.

I plunged through the gate, looked both ways, and ran after the plumes on the centurion's helmet. He walked fast, without looking back, and I knew he'd have been glad to lose me. But, you see, he was my only chance of dinner, and I was extremely hungry.

I bobbed along at the centurion's elbow for quite a time. He ignored me, but that was a lot better than cursing me or hitting me with his stick, so I was quite encouraged.

He turned a corner into yet another flint-guttered road and then he glanced sideways, sighed, and came to a halt.

'You're still here,' he said, resignedly.

'Yes, sir,' I said, bowing. 'At your service, Centurion.'

He sighed again.

'But I don't *want* any service,' he said. 'I have plenty of slaves and legionaries in my service already. I can't take on a boy who's going to need educating.'

I hastened to reassure him.

'Oh, there's no need to worry about that, sir,' I said. 'I'm perfectly content to be ignorant.'

He smiled wryly, but shook his head.

'And I'm strong, sir,' I went on. 'And very clever. And remarkably handsome.'

And very, *very* hungry.

'Why,' I went on, persuasively, 'anyone would be *glad* to have a boy like me around, sir.'

The centurion shook his head sadly.

'If only that were true,' he said. 'Well, come along. But be on your best behaviour because I'm going to introduce you to a lady.'

Actually, I was on my best behaviour already. I went along with him and hoped that the lady would give me some dinner.

The houses along this road were much smaller than the place where the magistrate had been, but they were still palaces compared with home. There was one building that looked a bit like a British house, but that turned out to have pigs in it.

Sabidus Maximus led me to a low house shaped like three sides of a square. Everything about it was ever so clean, and there was a girl of about my own age sitting on the doorstep. Her face lit up when she saw Sabidus, but she hardly deigned to glance at me.

'Is your mother home, Claudia?' asked Sabidus.

'Yes, Uncle.'

'Then run and tell her I'm here.'

The girl came back accompanied by a dark-haired woman with an anxious face. Sabidus introduced me. Sort of.

'Flavia Victorina,' he said. 'This is... er...'

'Lucan,' I said helpfully. I'd begun to think no one would ever ask.

'Lucan,' said Sabidus. 'He was a slave, but he's just been freed. And Tammonius Vitalis, bless him,' he went on, grimly, 'has given the boy into my care.'

'*Your* care?' said Flavia, blankly.

'It's a long story,' said Sabidus. 'The thing is, I don't know what to do with him. I can hardly take him back to the barracks with me.'

Flavia regarded me, and I, feeling sure I would soon faint with hunger, looked as attractive and deserving as I could.

'I don't know what Lepidus will make of it,' said Flavia, at last. 'Does the boy speak Latin?'

I'm a talented actor, so it was easy for me to look modest.

'A little, madam,' I said, smiling winningly.

Flavia looked even more doubtful.

'He has a barbarous accent,' she said. 'And he's very dirty.'

That was unfair, because I wasn't *very* dirty at all. I was just normally dirty. I mean, it was spring, so what did she expect? I washed quite often in summer, if we had an exceptionally warm day. And I had time.

'I suppose I'd better take him to the baths this afternoon,' said Sabidus, gloomily. 'When he's clean he may seem like a gift from the gods, Flavia Victorina.'

Flavia Victorina nodded, but suddenly looked very sad.

CHAPTER NINE

We Britons aren't savages – I mean, we always put new straw down on the ground before we sit down to eat – but honestly, those Romans were something else. They ate lying on their sides on benches, for a start. It was ever so uncomfortable. Their food was weird, too. I mean, they were obviously stinking rich – you should have seen their pottery bowls and glasses – but they ate *leaves*. I was so hungry I would have eaten anything, but the leaves were horrible.

If I was rich I'd have a pig killed every day, not stuff myself with leaves.

The girl Claudia didn't say much, but she made faces at me when no one was looking. I ignored her. Well, you don't bite the hand that feeds you, do you? And although the food was revolting it was better than starving. That house was like a dream. It had coloured walls, and swirls on the floor made of little squares of stone, and the whole place was *warm*, even though there was no fire. I didn't know anything about Roman gods – except for Nundina, bless her – but the power in that place was so strong it practically made my hair stand up on end.

Claudia's father was on his farm. It turned out that Flavia Victorina was my centurion's sister.

I was introduced to someone else at the end of the meal. There was an altar to a god called Lar right next to the table, and Flavia Victorina poured him some wine when we'd all finished. *Greetings, great Lar,* I prayed silently. *An honour to make your acquaintance.* Then Flavia told Claudia to take me away and find me a pot of oil and a strigil.

'What are you going to do, cook me?' I asked Claudia, as I followed her out.

She showed me her teeth.

'Yes,' she said fiercely. 'The meal was just to fatten you. When my father gets home he will hang you upside down and cut your throat, and then we will have you for dinner.'

I didn't believe her.

'What's a strigil?' I asked.

But she only snorted and flounced off and wouldn't talk to me anymore.

A strigil was quite like a little knife, but the oil jar Claudia gave me was so small you couldn't have fried much more than my big toe. Sabidus led me out into the town. I thought we were going to the baths, but first we went to a yard where there were a couple of rows of stone seats. Each one had a hole in the middle. People just hitched up their clothes, sat themselves down, and *went*. Just like that. Weird. And then they used oyster shells to scrape themselves clean. *Really* weird.

After that we did go to the baths. There was a courtyard with a pillared walk all around – the Romans really went in for those – and the first thing you had to do when you got inside was to take off all your clothes. I didn't like that one bit. A slave took our things and made marks on a tray of wax.

I don't think Romans feel the cold, because it was really perishing, and in the next room there were men right up to their necks in cold water. I practically died at the sight of it, but Sabidus led me to another room and that, thank all the gods, was quite warm. There were loads of men there, and everyone was rubbing handfuls of oil into their skin. Romans are just like Celts when they've got their clothes off, except they tend to be darker skinned, shorter, and hardly hairy at all.

When we were oily all over Sabidus led me to the next room. The heat in there was incredible. The room was so thick with steam that you could hardly see across it, and everyone was *drenched* in sweat. This was where the strigil came in.

You used it to scrape off all the dirt and sweat and stuff. It was quite fun – and it was amazing just how dirty I was. I got off loads, and even then Sabidus made me go all over myself again, because he said I was still filthy.

And, as it turned out, he was right.

Then came the best bit. There was a big pool of hot water to jump in, but we couldn't stay in long, because the place was so crowded. Sabidus sprinkled cold water over us. I didn't mind because I was so hot, and then we went back out into the oiling room again.

There was a guy howling like anything because he was having his underarm hair plucked. I was jolly glad to get away from there, but the next thing was almost as bad; Sabidus made me plunge into the cold bath. It wasn't as bad as I'd thought, though, because I was so hot that the cold never got in as far as my bones.

'Now you're beginning to look more like a Roman,' said Sabidus, when we were dressed again. But he didn't mean it nastily.

The courtyard was full of people chatting and gambling, and lots of them knew Sabidus. We watched a game called *soldiers*, which was played on a squared board, but I couldn't work out what it was all about. After a while the game must have finished because people paid each other money and the two players got up to go.

'Who's the boy, Sabidus Maximus?' asked a squat, stupid-looking man. He had a squat, stupid-looking boy with him, and they both had the sort of faces that looked much too pleased with themselves.

Sabidus answered so politely it was clear they were not friends.

'His name is Lucan, Gratus,' he said. 'The chief magistrate has given him into my care, but I'm hoping my sister will look after him for me.'

Gratus grinned.

'That's lucky,' he said. 'There's no other way your brother could manage to get a boy in his house.'

The little group around us fell suddenly silent, and I thought there was going to be a fight. I decided that when it started I'd go for Gratus's son. He was a bit taller than me, but he had an inviting, splodgy nose.

But Sabidus gave a thin smile and shook his head.

'I'm afraid you must excuse me, gentlemen,' he said. 'I have to preserve my strength for the emperor's service.'

I suppose when you're a centurion you can afford to swallow a few insults. I had to run to catch up with Sabidus as he strode off.

CHAPTER TEN

Claudia was sitting on a low wall in the garden when we got back to her house. She was singing to a clay figure.

'What are you singing to that thing for?' I asked.

I thought that was a reasonable question, but she flared up at once.

'It's got more sense than some people!' she said pointedly.

Well, I was beginning to feel hungry again, so instead of pushing her off the wall I sat down and tried to be friendly.

'There was a man called Gratus at the baths,' I told her. 'A *toenail* would have more sense than he has. And there was a boy with him with a face like a mouldy onion, and *he* looked worse than Gratus. I was going to hit him, but Sabidus towed me away.'

'That's Clementinus,' said Claudia. 'You should have hit him.'

'I will if you like,' I said. 'What's wrong with him?'

Claudia hesitated.

'He shouts things about... about me not having a brother,' she said.

I carried on being friendly and helpful. And to a Roman, too. I should have known that was going to be a waste of time.

'I'll say a prayer to Sul to make your mother fruitful, if you like,' I said. 'How many brothers do you want?'

Claudia looked at me and suddenly her eyes were blazing.

'Stupid filthy Celt!' she snapped. She got up and stalked off.

I hadn't a *clue* what I'd done wrong.

Flavia Victorina came out to find me a bit later on.

'Claudia came in very upset,' she said.

'All I did was offer to hit Clementinus,' I said. 'And to say a prayer for her.'

Romans don't light up a lot, but Flavia did smile, then.

'What did you offer to pray for, Lucan?'

'For some brothers for her.'

Flavia Victorina's smile faded at once.

'Claudia is ashamed of me,' she said sadly. 'I have offended the gods, somehow, and they will not give me a son.'

Well, that was *total* rubbish.

'You just need healing, that's all,' I said. But Flavia Victorina shook her head.

'Our gods have different ways,' she said. 'Now, you must come inside. My husband will be home soon. Marcus Lepidus will not be pleased if you keep him from his dinner.'

Marcus Lepidus Victor had grey hair, a scar running all the way down one cheek, and a no-nonsense manner. He was much older than his wife. He'd served in the army with Sabidus, and had been first centurion, which apparently was quite something.

He didn't think much of me. He said that my Latin was horrible and that I ate too much. Personally, I thought it was nice of me to eat anything at all, because it was leaves again. First we had oysters and *raw* leaves, and then we had meat in fish sauce with *cooked* leaves, and then we had some sweet bread-like stuff, which was so good that it took away the taste of all the rest.

Sabidus and Marcus Lepidus talked on and on about old times. I was just falling asleep when someone said 'Gratus,' and that woke me up.

Marcus Lepidus had stopped looking relaxed and happy.

'Gratus is a fool,' he said. 'I'm surprised no one's poisoned him.'

Claudia piped up.

'I will poison him for you, Father,' she offered. 'I know where there's a yew tree.'

I thought that Lepidus would snarl and lash out at her, but he only laughed, and thanked her, and told her, no. Even so, Flavia Victorina spoke quietly and seriously to Claudia for a long time.

'One day he'll get his comeuppance,' went on Lepidus. 'But I'm afraid it's beneath my dignity to attend to him.'

Sabidus waved to one of the waiting slaves for more wine.

'And mine, too, unfortunately,' he said. 'It's almost enough to make me wish I was a legionary again.'

Lepidus smiled, and shook his head.

'Oh no you don't,' he said. 'You wouldn't want to dig roads and sleep eight to a room again.'

And the conversation slipped back to the old times he and Sabidus had shared.

I woke up next morning and for a moment I thought I'd died and been taken by the gods. I was lying under a blanket on a stuffed soft sack, and a stranger was pulling back a cloth to reveal a glass window through which I could see a clear blue sky.

As if that wasn't enough, the stranger had brought me breakfast: the softest bread, and the sweetest apple, that I'd ever dreamed of.

After breakfast I tried to find my way out into the garden, but I got lost and ended up at the little shrine where the god Lar lived. So I knelt down and asked him to find me a home where my talents would be properly appreciated.

When I got up I found Claudia watching me.

'Were you cursing us?' she asked.

'Of course not,' I said, annoyed. I really do *not* do curses. 'I was asking if I could go somewhere where people are friendly, that's all.'

She blinked thoughtfully.

'I hope you can,' she said. 'Perhaps Uncle Sabidus will take you to Isca Silurum with him. One of the soldiers there might want you. There might be one who's not fussy.'

I was getting really fed up with Claudia.

'Are you Romans always so polite to guests?' I asked.

She shrugged.

'Well, why *would* anyone want you?' she asked. 'Round here we don't like people who eat people.'

'I've never eaten anybody in my life!'

'Well, your people do. And you're all dirty and ignorant. And you go around fighting all the time.'

That was a bit rich, coming from a Roman.

'And how about your lot?' I asked. 'What about your legions? They're not exactly peaceful, are they?'

'That's only at first, if people don't appreciate what we're doing for them,' she explained. 'Once people see what we're like they soon become quite peaceful and contented, like the people are here.'

'Oh yes,' I said sarcastically. 'Like the people in my mother's tribe's lands. Peacefully dead. How many people did you kill during Boudicca's rebellion, Claudia?'

I knew it was thousands upon thousands. My mother told me once that all the lands where her family used to live were deserted, now.

'And how many did *your* people kill?' Claudia demanded, in return. 'You Celts wiped out Verulanium and Londinium. You even killed the women and the children.' I hadn't known that. I stopped for a minute.

'I've never killed anyone,' I said, at last.

'And neither have I.'

We both looked at each other for a moment, and then I sat down thoughtfully.

'At least we don't watch people being torn to bits by wild animals,' I said.

'It's better than stuffing them inside wicker cages and setting fire to them, like you do.'

I shook my head at once.

'My people don't do that. That's the Druids. I've never even *seen* a Druid.'

'They're still Celts.'

'Yes,' I agreed. 'And your great emperor is Roman, isn't he? And I've heard some funny tales about *him*, too.'

That made Claudia stop and think. Then she sat down next to me.

'I suppose it wouldn't be *that* bad if you stayed here with us for a while,' she said. 'Mother would like a boy to fuss over. And Uncle Sabidus would be pleased to be rid of you. And I suppose it'd be company.'

She was right. It wouldn't be that bad if I stayed for a while. Claudia was a bit of a pain, but I got plenty of food, even if half of it was leaves. In any case, it was a lot safer to be friends with Claudia than enemies. I didn't want to be poisoned with yew berries, did I?

'Father doesn't think much of you,' Claudia went on, thoughtfully. 'But Mother might just persuade him to let you stay. Heaven knows why, but she quite likes you.'

'Of course heaven knows why,' I told her. 'Why, I've prayed to every god I've ever heard of to save me from being tortured to death by you lot.'

'We don't torture people to death! Well, not as a rule. Only if it's necessary. We're very peaceful people. Peaceful and organised.'

'I know,' I said. 'That's another reason why I don't mind staying.'

CHAPTER ELEVEN

I knew Claudia was a dangerous enemy. What I hadn't realised was that she was a dangerous friend, as well.

She laid plans.

'Father likes manly boys,' she said. 'Look, I've got Father's spare sword from his chest. Go into the courtyard and pretend you're fighting with it. Father's bound to see you.'

Marcus Lepidus saw me, all right. He strode out, took the sword from me, and whacked me with it for taking it without permission.

Claudia was rather pleased.

'That's one up to you,' she said. 'You hardly yelled at all when he hit you. He'll like that. Now go and do it again.'

'*What?* You must be joking,' I said, rubbing myself.

She wasn't. She said it would prove I was determined and brave. In the end we compromised. I *did* go and play at sword-fighting again, but I did it with a cabbage-stalk instead of a sword. Marcus Lepidus saw me again, but this time when he came out he showed me how to hold a sword properly, and what you did with your feet when you lunged.

Sabidus was really annoyed with me when he heard about the sword, but Marcus Lepidus told him I'd already been taken care of.

'I'm sorry the boy has caused you trouble,' said Sabidus, gloomily.

'Boys are always trouble,' said Marcus Lepidus.

Claudia was full of ideas. After lunch, when Flavia Victorina had poured out the offering to Lar, Claudia led me to a room where there were wax masks hanging on the wall. Well, I'm really brave, as you know, but those masks had glowing glass eyes and I didn't like them one bit.

'What are they?' I asked.

'The death masks of my ancestors,' said Claudia. Even she spoke in a low voice. 'If you want to join the household then you'd better introduce yourself.'

Well, those masks gave me the heebie jeebies so I prayed to them really hard. I definitely wanted them on my side.

I asked Claudia if there were any other Roman gods who might help me, and it turned out they had some that were especially interested in children. There was Cunina, who guarded your bed; Ossipago, who made your bones grow straight and strong; and Interduca, who watched you on your way to school.

'Oh, I won't bother with school,' I said.

'You'll have to. All Roman boys go,' pointed out Claudia.

I shook my head.

'I'm not interested in scratching things in wax,' I said. 'I'd rather be a soldier, like Sabidus and Marcus Lepidus.'

'Then you'll *have* to go to school,' said Claudia, triumphantly. 'You can't be a legionary unless you can read. So there!'

There was another god, called Levana, who was in charge of the time when a father first lifts his child in his arms. I wondered if my own father had done something like that, long ago, and I wished I could remember him.

There was a performance at the amphitheatre that afternoon, and Claudia nagged Sabidus until he and Marcus Lepidus said they would take us.

'But put your toga on properly, Lucan,' he said irritably. 'That tunic's hardly fit for a dish cloth.'

The show took place outside in a flat area with a high bank all around it where people sat on benches to watch.

'What's it going to be like?' I asked Claudia, as we went to our seats. I was just about the only person wearing a toga and I almost wished I'd stayed at home.

'There'll be gladiators, I expect,' she said. 'And a wild bull. I heard they'd got a bear, as well, but I don't suppose they'll let it out today because there's not much of a crowd.'

'Here,' said Marcus Lepidus, shoving a coin into my hand. 'Go and buy us some cakes from that man down there. And don't be all day about it.'

It took me ages to fight my way past everyone's legs and get down to ground level, and of course by that time the cake man had wandered off. When I finally spotted him he was over on the other side of a grassy passage bordered by two fences. Luckily I'm an excellent climber so that didn't bother me. I got over the first fence with no trouble at all, and only quite a small rip to my toga.

The first thing I noticed when I jumped down onto the grass was that someone had left a heap of old clothes by the side of the fence.

And then I looked again and saw it was Aphrodisius.

'Hello,' I said. 'What are you doing here?' He clutched my knees and started gibbering that he was going to die.

'Die?' I echoed. 'What makes you think you're going to die?'

I should have guessed. No one had wanted to buy the poor fool when he'd been put up for sale, and so he was being used as a gladiator. That meant he was going to be given a sword and put into the arena. Then a man called a retiarius, armed with a net, trident and dagger, would come and kill him.

I thought of telling Aphrodisius that *he* might kill the *retiarius*, but that was so unlikely it hardly seemed kind to mention it. I also wondered about telling him to put up such a brilliant fight that the crowd would ask for him to be spared – but there was hardly any chance of that, either. I was just patting his scrawny back and saying 'There, there,' when a shadow fell over us.

'Is your best friend going to die, then?' it said.

Clementinus was looking over the fence at us.

'Go away,' I said, wishing I knew more Latin so I could say it more strongly. Clementinus spat.

'They've got a stretcher all ready for your friend's corpse,' he jeered. 'I bet he gets it right in the middle of his –'

'Go *away,*' I said, again. But Clementinus was enjoying himself.

'It's going to be agony,' he said. 'First he'll get his –'

I got up, grabbed Clementinus by the front of his tunic, and pulled him over the fence. Then I hit him.

I'd been looking forward to hitting Clementinus, but it was impossible to do it properly because he crumpled into a ball at once and started shrieking. I was just trying to turn him over when someone called my name.

It was Claudia, up on the mound. She slithered down the grass slope and the next thing I knew she'd climbed the fence and was looking down at us.

'What are you doing down there?' she asked. 'Father's ever so cross. He thinks you've run off with his money.'

'Of course I haven't,' I said, distracted. 'But Aphrodisius is going to be thrown into the arena to fight to the death and I don't know what to do.'

'Oh. What's Clementinus doing?'

I looked round. Clementinus had uncurled himself and was crawling stealthily away. Good riddance, as far as I was concerned.

'How can we get Aphrodisius out of here?' I asked.

'You can't,' said Claudia. 'Forget it. And more to the point, how are you going to get *yourself* out of there?'

It hadn't occurred to me until then, but the fences were smooth and unclimbable from my side. I was just wondering what to do when there was a bray of trumpets and then a cheer. Claudia looked up so sharply she nearly fell off the fence. Then she reached out a hand to me.

'I'll pull you up,' she said.

The ground was beginning to shake under my sandals as though someone was hitting the ground with a mallet. Clementinus and Aphrodisius looked round wildly, squawked, and leapt to their feet.

'You'd never be able to pull me up,' I said to Claudia. 'I'm much too –'

'Quick!' said Claudia, suddenly as white as her tunic.

I looked round at them all. They were all terrified.

'Look,' I said. 'Just *what* is going on?'

Then something began making a noise like a pair of bellows and Clementinus jumped a foot in the air and grabbed hold of Claudia's hand – but of course all he succeeded in doing was pulling her down on top of the rest of us. And I still didn't know what all the panic was about.

Up on the mound someone shouted something, and the shout was taken up by others. They'd all turned to stare further along the grassy strip – and when I followed their gaze, I finally understood.

They'd released the wild bull. And it was in with us.

CHAPTER TWELVE

Clementinus took one look, squawked again, and threw himself, scrabbling wildly, at the fence. He got three feet up and then he slid down again, his fingernails scraping the wood all the way.

The bull was lithe and black. It looked mean.

I stood there for a moment listening to my heart beating. Aphrodisius was running round in circles going, 'Ooh, ooh,' and it wasn't until he trod on my toe that my brain stopped screaming, 'Nooooo!' and started working. We had to get out of there. I grabbed Aphrodisius as he went by on his fourth circuit, shook some sense into him, and then between us we managed to bundle Claudia up over the fence. I'm naturally really brave like that. Then I noticed that someone was jumping up and down squealing, 'Me next!' in my ear, so we bundled Clementinus over as well. I might have left Clementinus to get gored by the bull if I'd had time to think, but things were just happening so fast.

The bull fixed his angry red eyes on me, stamped, and charged. I went to run, tripped over the end of my stupid toga, fell, and rolled, somehow managing to leave my toga behind me. Luckily the bull went for the toga. It tossed and ripped it horribly, but before it could turn back to finish us off I'd at least had time to get to my feet.

I'd seen men fighting bulls at the cattle gatherings at home, so I knew the tricks; well, I knew them in theory, anyway. There were loads of people shouting all round, and a little way away a man had jumped over the fence onto the grassy strip, but I'd snatched up what remained of my toga and I was too busy watching the bull to take much notice.

I'm ever so brave, obviously, but I think that if I'd had more time I'd have been a bit worried. That bull looked so *mean*. It charged at me, but at the last minute I sidestepped and the bull went through with the toga on its horns, snorting and half-blinkered. I'd meant to whisk away the toga at the last minute, but that bull was even faster than I'd thought.

What next? The bull was turning in a tight circle, kicking up divots of mud.

I suddenly realised there wasn't anything I *could* do next. Then someone seized me. It was Sabidus Maximus.

'Quick!' he bellowed. Aphrodisius was nowhere to be seen, but Marcus Lepidus was up on the fence. Sabidus half threw me up, Marcus Lepidus swung me round, and I found myself falling down onto a jumble of other people's arms and legs. Then someone tumbled down on top of me, and I knocked my head, and after that I just lay quietly and watched the stars slide past.

After a while, people began to untangle themselves and get up.

'Lucan!' said someone. 'Are you all right?'

I was still trying to work out what day it was, so I hadn't got any spare brains left to answer a difficult question like that. Someone lifted me up. It was a man with a scarred face. I had an idea that I'd probably seen him somewhere before.

'He saved my life,' someone was saying breathlessly. 'Did you see, Father? He saved me and Clementinus!'

'Yes, yes,' said the scarred man, with a sigh. 'I saw, sure enough. Very well, very well, I admit defeat. My family I can withstand, but this time fate has vanquished me.'

The man put an arm round my shoulder. I was really surprised. I still hadn't quite worked out who he was, but I'd never have put him down as the affectionate type.

'We'll go to the Temple of Levana tomorrow, and there we will make sacrifices to the goddess Levana,' he said, resignedly. 'And after that I shall be your father.'

Everyone around me started looking terribly pleased, so I thought I'd better look pleased, too.

It was funny, because I had a faint idea that my father had been someone else entirely.

'I think the poor boy is still dazed,' said someone, after a while.

'Food,' said the scarred man, decidedly. 'That's what the boy needs.'

The scarred man summoned a pedlar who was going by with a tray of cakes – and when I saw the pedlar's face I suddenly remembered everything, because it was Balbus.

I don't think Balbus was all that happy to see me being doted on by a rich Roman family, but he sold us the cakes anyway.

'Be honest, and honour the gods, and you will prosper,' Sabidus told Balbus, through a mouthful.

Balbus took the money, scowled, and stomped off. That was the last time I saw Balbus – but he was cunning, and I bet he got rich again. Whether he got honest, I wouldn't like to say.

The cake soon made me feel better, so as we'd paid to get in we went to see what was left of the circus.

The first act after we got to our seats was a gladiator.

'*That's* a gladiator?' I asked Claudia, because that man must have been the scrawniest, weediest gladiator in the history of the Roman empire.

Then I looked again and saw that it was Aphrodisius.

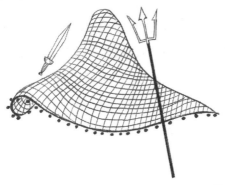

CHAPTER THIRTEEN

Aphrodisius was not only weedy, but he was also the biggest coward I've ever come across in my entire life. They had to drag him into the arena and then, when his opponent the retiarius came out, Aphrodisius took one look, jumped in the air, and started running as fast as he could. He ran very upright, with his hands by his sides and his large feet splayed out, and all the retiarius could do was chase after him.

Unfortunately the retiarius was weighed down with his trident and he couldn't catch Aphrodisius. They had to get extra men to come and try to corner him. But Aphrodisius was as fast as a greased weasel with fear, and the extra men just tripped each other up. So then the men who were employed to carry off the bodies came on as well, and eventually, after a lot of falling over and bumping into each other, they did manage to catch Aphrodisius.

And then the purple, puffing retiarius got out his dagger and looked round for permission from the crowd to deliver the final blow.

I couldn't look.

I'm sure a Roman audience would have given Aphrodisius the 'thumbs down' sign for death but most of that crowd had been born Celts, and they were all laughing so much they only just had the strength to wave their handkerchiefs to stop the execution.

Aphrodisius, the biggest coward in Britain, left the arena with the applause ringing in his ears.

Claudia and I tried our best to persuade Marcus Lepidus to buy Aphrodisius, but Marcus Lepidus had too much sense for that. So then we tried to persuade Sabidus.

'He *did* help save my life,' pointed out Claudia. 'And it seems ungrateful to leave him to his fate.'

I think Claudia could have worn Sabidus Maximus down in the end, but he had to leave to rejoin his legion the next day and so she didn't have time. But Aphrodisius ended up all right, because so many people talked about how funny he'd been that Tammonius Vitalis, the magistrate, bought him as a clown.

It was a good thing Aphrodisius didn't end up in our household, really, because he was a lazy, no-good liar. Still, it was funny to see him swaggering about. Aphrodisius thought that being the slave of the chief magistrate made him the finest thing in town, and after a while he hardly deigned to speak to me.

So that's how I became a Roman. It's all right. I mean, I'm well fed and comfortable – except at school, which is barbaric – and my mother and father are all right, mostly. Since I saved Clementinus from the bull he and his father leave us alone.

The only things I really miss are the Celtic stories people used to sing round the fire, about how evil the Romans are.

Still, I'm getting used to being a Roman. Sometimes, when I wake up snug and warm in my bed, I remember the stone hut I used to live in.

And, just for a moment, I think I'm in the land of the gods.

BONUS BITS!

Who were the Celts?

Between about 750 BC and 12 BC the Celts were the most powerful people in central and northern Europe. They lived in tribes.

The word 'Celt' comes from a Greek word 'keltoi', which means 'barbarians'.

The British Celts lived in roundhouses. We know about these as remains of them have been found during archaeological digs.

Who were the Romans?

The Romans became the dominant power in Europe when Julius Caesar led his Roman legions to conquer Gaul (now mainly France) and then, in 55 BC, attacked Britain. Julius Caesar didn't stay in Britain for long, but 100 years later the Romans attacked Britain again and this time they settled.

Where are the places in the story?

Lots of real places are mentioned in this story, although you probably don't know them by their Roman names. Here is a whistle-stop tour of them!

Viroconium – This was a Roman town. At its peak it was believed to be the 4th largest Roman settlement in Britain with a population of more than 15,000 people. It was roughly in what is now Wroxeter, Shropshire.

The Spring of Sul – This can still be seen in what is now the city of Bath. In Roman times, Bath was called 'Aquae Sulis', which means 'the Waters of Sul'.

Calleva Atrebatum – This was an Iron Age settlement that then became a Roman town, near Silchester in what is now Hampshire. There are still ruins that can be seen today and are known as Silchester Roman Town.

Carthage – This is a city in Tunisia. The Romans destroyed the city in 146 BC. However, the Romans then rebuilt Carthage and it became the Roman empire's fourth most important city.

Isca Silurum – This was the site of a Roman fortress and settlement. It is in the outskirts of modern-day Newport, South Wales, and its remains can still be seen today. It had a large amphitheatre.

Verulanium – This was a Roman town. Its remains can still be seen today in St Albans, Hertfordshire.

Londinium – This was a major centre for business and shopping in Roman times. It stood on the site of the current City of London.

What does that mean?

There are lots of words in this story that are specific to Roman times (which is hardly surprising, as the story is set in those times!). This list might help you if you get stuck.

Latin – the language of ancient Rome and its empire

homestead – a farmhouse and outbuildings

beast of burden – an animal like a donkey or mule that carries heavy things

toga – a loose piece of clothing worn by the people of ancient Rome. It was made of a single piece of cloth and covered the whole body apart from the right arm

denarii – Roman silver coins

centurion – a commander in the Roman army

basilica – a large, rectangular hall or building that was used in the Roman empire for official events and as a law court

merchant – a person who sells things

strigil – a curved metal tool that was used by the

Romans to scrape sweat and dirt from their skin in a hot-air bath

amphitheatre – a circular or oval building that had no roof, used for sport and drama events. It had seats up the sides in tiers for people to watch the action in the middle of the ring

gladiator – a man who fought with weapons against other men or wild animals for people to watch

retiarius – a gladiator who used a net to trap his opponent

Boudicca's Battles

In the story Lucan and Claudia argue about Boudicca. But who was she?

The Iceni tribe lived in what is now East Anglia. They were Celts but their king was a friend of the Romans. When he died, he left half his kingdom to his two daughters, and the other half to the Roman emperor.

The Romans wanted to have all of the kingdom so they treated Boudicca and her daughters very badly. They wanted her to give up her throne. They also demanded extra taxes.

The Iceni tribe were angry and other Celtic tribes came to join them in their fight against the Romans. They marched to the capital of Roman Britain, Camulodunum (which is now Colchester in Essex), and attacked the town. They burned the new Roman temple.

Boudicca and her tribe then continued on and she led her army towards Londinium. The Romans did not have enough people to fight the Celts and so they fled. The Celts burned the city and killed hundreds of people (both Celts and Romans).

The Iceni then decided to move on and attack Verulanium. The Roman governor, Paulinus, prepared for battle and called for more soldiers. The Roman commander in Isca Dumnoniorum (which is now Exeter) refused to send more so Paulinus had to fight with what he had. Boudicca had ten times more people than Paulinus but the

Roman army was very well trained.

There was a huge battle – the Romans won and therefore the only reports we have come from the Roman side! Many of the Celts were killed and Boudicca drank poison to kill herself rather than be captured by the Romans.

What Next?

This story gives us lots of information about life in Roman times. Why not do some research to find out more? Choose a question and use books and the internet to answer it. Think about how you could present your answers – in a written, spoken, video or visual presentation – you choose!

You might have your own questions based on this story or you could make a start with one of these:

- What was life like as a slave to a Roman master?
- How did the Romans train their army?
- What did Roman baths look like?
- Would you have liked to be a Roman child?

**Did you enjoy Lucan's story?
Then look out for these other
adventures in ancient history!**

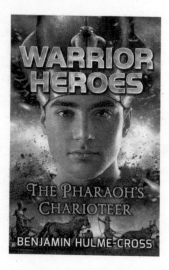

ISBN: 9781472925893

ISBN: 9781472925923

Join brothers Arthur and
Finn as they travel back to
ancient Egypt to discover
dangerous rivalries and a
prince and princess with
strong opinions. Can they
prevent a kidnapping
and stop a war?

Travel back in time with
Arthur and Finn to help
one Spartan soldier save
his family before facing
his final battle. Can they
impress the Spartan king
and avoid the wrath of
the Persian Army?